CW00787180

Higher,higher, till he seemed to be floating ever more into the blue

BOOK TWO

Mo's Strange Adventure

by

BRIDGET A. CLARK

MOCAT SERIES

SPIRE CITY
PUBLISHING

MOCAT SERIES

Mo's Strange Adventure

First Impression   2002

Copyright © 2002 ISBN 1-904208-01-0

Published by Spire City Publishing

Northern Office
7 Denbigh Drive
Clitheroe
Lancs
BB7 2BH
Tel\Fax 01200 428 823

Printed by Information Press

Southfield Road
Eynsham
Oxford
OX29 1JJ

Cover by Blenheim Colour

Southfield Road
Eynsham
Oxford
OX29 4JB

MOCAT SERIES
Book Two

Mo's Strange Adventure
CONTENTS

Intoduction

Illustrations by the Author

Mocat Series

There are TEN books in the Mocat Series
This book is the Second in the Series

1 Dorinda's Clever Cat (Available)
   ISBN 1-904208-00-2
2 Mo's Strange Adventure (Available)
   ISBN 1-904208-01-0

To be Published

3 Mo takes a Holiday
4 Dorinda's Magic Mirrors
5 A Journey for Dorinda
6 Puzzles for Dorinda
7 Mo and the Haunted Castle
8 Mo and Midsummer Magic
9 Mo and the Black Pearl
10 Dorinda and the Sad Princess

INTRODUCTION

MO's STRANGE ADVENTURE

Once upon a time there was a cat called Mauleverer (Mo for short) who lived in a palace with a princess called Dorinda. Mo blamed himself for letting her fall asleep on her sixteenth birthday after seeing a box of pills on a television set. This was because a spell had been cast on her by her wicked relative the witch Henbane, who had smuggled the television set into the palace. Mo thinks that if he had got to Dorinda before Henbane all would now be well. But things are not well. Dorinda, the king and queen, and all the inhabitants of the palace are fast asleep. Only Mo was left awake on the day of the spell because he was fast asleep under a blanket in a laundry basket and it missed him.

Now read on...........

CHAPTER ONE

A New Day

Dawn broke over the sleeping palace. There was no birdsong, no stir of life. Not even the leaves on the trees fluttered. There was no breeze, and no life in the palace: no milkmen, no clatter of dishes, no maids running about their duties, no busy servants in and out of the palace kitchens. The only sound that could be heard was that of gentle snoring as the king, his councillors, his footmen, his men at arms and all the rest of the palace family and staff slept on.

As the sun rose Mo stirred, opened his eyes, and listened. But for what? There was no sound at all in the laundry room, no boiler being lit, no chatter of washerwomen, no dragging of baskets along the floors.

'Oh dear! Oh dear! Poor Dorinda! And it was all my fault!'

For Mo blamed himself for what had happened. He had left the princess at an important time (he had had pressing problems). And the sleeping spell had been cast all over everyone and everything in the palace. He had been safe from it, covered as he was by blankets, snug in his laundry basket, but - poor Dorinda!

He considered he had seriously neglected his duty.

Mo made his way, a troubled, silent black shape, to the Kitchen where he found the head cook, who liked to make his breakfast. But instead there she was totally still in the act of icing Dorinda's birthday cake, the icing tube in a hand raised high. Ysa, the scullery maid was turning blue amid her soapsuds as she knelt, frozen, on the floor she was scrubbing.

Sadly Mo wandered out of the kitchen through the green baize door and along the corridor to the oak door that led to the Great Hall of the palace. It was all still as he had left it yesterday. There was Lady Fawn, holding her little poodle; Lord Jonquil with his prized set of bagpipes; there was the Arabian prince; the Lord

In walked a large shape all green and yellow

Chamberlain, a statue amongst several other statues, as he inspected the invitations list of Dorinda's birthday guests.

Mo was just about to climb the stairs to go to Dorinda's bedroom and see how she was, when he heard footsteps outside the Great Door. He froze - who could it be? Everybody was asleep! He grew even more alarmed when he heard a key turn in the lock. Who had a key to the door he had locked himself last night?

The door opened. In walked a large shape all green and yellow, clouds of silk and chiffon swirling. A pale, almost silvery face, piercing blue eyes, thick white eyebrows, and all of this topped by white hair that looked like the ice cream in an ice cream cornet.

"Aunt Daffodil!" said Mo.

"Indeed!" said the shape.

"Er", blushed Mo, for he had remembered something.

"If it's about my picture, don't worry" said Aunt Daffodil. "I know all about it. What I've actually come for is the rocking-horse. No need to come with me" she said, as she crossed the Hall. "I'll bring it down myself."

The rocking-horse only stood two feet high but Mo was too small to carry it and Aunt Daffodil was a strong woman. She could, at a pinch, manage a rocking-horse.

"I'll pop in on Dorinda on my way down. You stay here, mind, till I come back."

Mo would not dream of disobeying anyone so important as Aunt Daffodil. He was not really surprised by her arrival, for she always knew everything that was going on. He felt a little bit more cheerful. Aunt Daffodil would help in his terrible situation - she was Dorinda's favourite auntie. She did not seem cross about her portrait either. (This had got a bit of a battering). So Mo, feeling heartened, waited till she came back, curling himself upon a cushion that the Arabian prince had brought with him.

Soon Aunt Daffodil was back, carrying the rocking-horse under her arm. (A very strong woman).

"Now, Mo, we have to make the best of this. I have a plan to sort it all out.

But you have to help me."

"Is Dorinda all right?" asked Mo.

"As right as can be, in the circumstances. We must take action now, for her sake, and try to get everything back to normal."

Mo nodded. Aunt Daffodil did not seem to be blaming him at all, for which he was grateful.

Still carrying the rocking-horse she walked to the door. Her car was parked a little way down the palace forecourt.

"Picquot!" She signalled to her chauffeur.

Picquot appeared at the car door in a twinkling.

"Take this horse and put it in the boot!" she said. So Picquot did what he was told, tucking the horse under his arm and walking to the back of the car.

Take this horse and put it in the boot

"Now you and I, Mo, must lock this place up again and go to my house. We'll stop at a restaurant along the way and I'll explain what we have to do."

So the palace door was locked on its sleeping inhabitants and Mo and Aunt Daffodil got into the car.

Silence was all round them for about 30 kilometres.

Then the world seemed to wake up again. People were chatting in doorways, farmers were driving carts along the road, women were trudging along with shopping baskets.

'So we're out of the spell', thought Mo.

Aunt Daffodil started to look tired. Mo guessed she was not feeling very well. She got travel sick, and could only make journeys in small hops.

There was an inn coming up on the left. 'The Troll's Head' said the sign, which displayed a picture of a very handsome troll with huge side whiskers.

"Pull in here, Picquot", said Aunt Daffodil. "We'll all have lunch." She had travelled far enough.

Mo and Aunt Daffodil walked into the inn dining-room. A tray was ordered for Picquot with his lunch and his favourite beer on it (not too much beer because he was driving).

Mo and Aunt Daffodil sat down at a little corner table set for two, with a white cloth on it and a little vase of small flowers. They could see out of the window into a pleasant garden. A troll waiter in black and white uniform was waiting to take their order.

A very handsome troll

"I'll only have a little piece of toast" said Aunt Daffodil, who had been to this restaurant many times before.

She ordered fish for Mo. Mo would have liked to order for himself, but he let Aunt Daffodil do it.

When it came it was very nice, a beautiful piece of fish with cheese stuffing.

Mo and Aunt Daffodil had a glass of lemonade each.

"Now, Mo", she said. "I have something to put to you."

Mo fixed his eyes on her face.

"This business of Dorinda." Aunt Daffodil went on. "I was looking at the screen last night (Aunt Daffodil used a screen rather than a crystal ball - it gave a clearer picture which did not curve at the edges). "I must confess I was wondering whatever I could do next."

She paused.

"Well, I was looking at the screen, watching a picture of you - I saw you on the birthday all the time and watched you seeing to Dorinda. Great what you did with those gnomes!" She gave a little laugh. Then her face grew more serious.

"Then I saw something completely different."

Pause again.

"Now Mo, I have something to put to you"

"You were sitting on Dorinda's rocking-horse."

"I have never been on Dorinda's rocking-horse" said Mo.

"You were on the rocking-horse" went on Aunt Daffodil, "and what is more, you were on it in a desert."

"In a desert!" exclaimed Mo. "What was I doing in a desert?"

He had been on different holidays with Dorinda but he couldn't recall actually being in a desert. A bit of sand near the pyramids, that was all.

"You were in a desert" said Aunt Daffodil. "Note - I was looking into the future, not

7

catching up on the present or the past."

Mo didn't like the sound of this. He didn't like watery places but he certainly didn't fancy a desert.

"So" went on Aunt Daffodil. "I decided I had to get you over to my house with the rocking-horse, work a bit of magic on you far away from old Henbane's spell and then see if you could get to that desert. I would go myself, but you know my travel sickness would allow Henbane to get at me. And if you went I could see from home that everything was all right at both ends of the journey."

Mo found the fish didn't taste so nice any more. He knew he wouldn't like that desert. But then a little voice in his head told him that perhaps in the desert he'd find a chance to make up for his mistake yesterday. So he turned to Aunt Daffodil and said "Let's go!".

---

ooOoo

CHAPTER TWO.

The desert

On reaching her house Aunt Daffodil lost no time in taking Mo to her lounge with the french windows. Picquot followed her in with the rocking-horse.

"Set it facing the windows" said Aunt Daffodil as she opened them. "Now, Mo, climb on his back."

So Mo climbed up onto the back of the rocking-horse.

Aunt Daffodil then opened a little cupboard in the corner of her room. "Here is a little bag for you to carry some food in. I know how hungry you get."

Mo felt at that moment he could never eat again. The thought of what might be waiting in the desert quite put him off the idea of food.

"Look in the bag" said Aunt Daffodil. "It's got tuna sandwiches in. Your favourite."

The bag was on a long strap which she fastened over Mo's shoulder.

Then Aunt Daffodil stepped back - drew a circle round Mo on the rocking-horse, went to the cupboard again and took out a wand. She waved it three times, muttered something Mo couldn't hear and then gave him and the horse a hearty tap with it. She said

"Dorinda sleeps. The desert creeps.

And Mo my knight his faith he keeps."

Sparks flew from the wand. And suddenly Mo found himself whizzing out of the room through the french windows, out across the garden, over the wall, higher, higher till he seemed to be floating evermore into the blue.....

Then everything went black.

Bump! The rocking-horse had landed! Everything around was still very dark. Was he in the desert now? Mo wondered. His unspoken thought was answered as a pale moon appeared, suddenly shining in the midst of the gloom. He was indeed surrounded by sand, which seemed to stretch in every direction as far as his eyes could see, long, level, silver. The horse's rockers were gradually sinking into it. It seemed to be stuck, unable to move at all.

'What to do?' thought Mo.

He climbed off the horse and tried to pull it with his arms around its neck. Nothing happened.

'But even if I could pull it' thought Mo, 'What direction should I be going in?'

Every direction including the one the horse was facing seemed to be leading nowhere. Nothing but sand....

Mo looked at the direction he was facing from the front of the horse looking back. Black clouds seemed to now to be moving around the horizon. He strained his eyes to watch them. They changed their shapes as Mo watched. First they seemed to be a forest full of pine trees, then they shifted again, and became a fold of hills, then changed again and became a.... castle? They made a very solid-looking castle; the moon-light gave it the effect of windows with eerie light coming from them in ghostly rays.

They made a very solid looking castle

'I'll go there' thought Mo. 'I'll get the horse to turn round.'

But the horse wouldn't budge. It was im-movable, no matter how hard Mo pulled and tugged. And the rockers were sinking even deeper into the sand.

He could just see another shape sitting on the sand behind the horse. And then another, and another. Huge black birds that just sat looking at his struggles. Mo felt a bit uneasy.

'Vultures! That's what they are! Vultures!'

Mo knew it was no good trying to fight with birds as big as vultures. They didn't bother about fighting anyway. They just hung around, waiting....

He tugged at the horse's reins. He scrabbled at the sand around the rockers. As fast as he moved sand away it all dribbled back.

"I'm not going to go in that direction" said Mo aloud. "castle or no castle, and that's flat!".

No sooner had he said this than the horse gave a jerk - as though it had been waiting for Mo to decide. Its rockers suddenly shook free and Mo was able to pull it over the sand a little way.

'The castle was in the wrong direction after all. Let's go opposite to it!'

Mo pulled the horse. It slid along the sand quite easily. He did not try to get on its back and ride it. He just let it point him the way he was to go. From time to time he looked back. The vultures were still there, but as he was travelling quite well now they were soon out of sight.

After a while little tufts of grass were becoming visible through the sand.

'Getting better' thought Mo. He trudged on and soon there were dunes, with heather and bracken. And after the dunes the sand was no more. The darkness was lightening too, and soon it was dawn and then broad daylight. Mo continued to walk on for at least an hour. At last before him Mo saw a level field of mossy turf - and beyond that - Mo could hardly believe his eyes - a river! (Not that he was keen on rivers, but there were little boats with people in them, and motor boats with cabins built on them.

And over the river was a little bridge. Some children were crossing it. On the other side of the bridge was - a railway station! With a platform and a signal, and a guard in blue uniform!

Mo pulled the horse close to the bridge to see the sign that told the name of the railway company. 'Clock Railway inc' it said. Mo didn't know what 'inc' was but he was quite happy to have reached some sort of civilisation at last.

He saw the children crossing the bridge and coming nearer. There were six in all, three of them quite small, two boys and a girl all dressed in cream jackets and cream trousers, with cream square collars. As they came closer Mo noticed something unusual - on their backs printed on the cream cloth were numbers in white. One boy had a five, the girl had a six, and the other boy had seven. The three other children were much bigger. They were dressed in green jackets and trousers and had a kind of badge, which looked to Mo to be similar to a sprig of holly. One boy had the number 13 on his back, another 14, and one 15. All of them were whooping and laughing.

When they reached Mo they behaved as though they didn't see him at all.

"Hallo" said Mo.

And over the river was a little bridge

"Yippee! A horse! A horse! My computer for a horse!"said the biggest boy, whereupon all the big boys grabbed the rocking-horse and tried to pull it away from Mo.

"Don't do that!" shrieked Mo.

But the children took no notice. Mo was dragged away from the horse and forced to leave go of its reins, while laughing and giggling the boys took the reins and pulled the horse along. The smaller children deliberately made a barrier between Mo and the boys so he couldn't get near the horse. He was smaller even than the boy with 5 on his back.

Mo watched his horse surrounded by the group of children being pulled along to the bridge, dragged over it and towards the railway. Then he could see the entrance to a kind of subway where they all went in order to take the horse to the other side of the railway line.

Mo rushed across the bridge to follow it. Too late! As he got to the station platform the last he saw of his horse was of it disappearing down a long street of terrace houses that stood at right angles to the railway line. He could not see exactly where and when it disappeared. But it was gone! Of that there was no doubt!

Mo felt a bit upset. Now he had no transport and how could he tell Aunt Daffodil Dorinda's horse was missing!

ooOoo

He could see the entrance to a kind of subway

CHAPTER THREE

On the Train

Mo decided it was time to follow the children down the street. There was an entry to the street from the railway station. He was just about to go to it when a group of passengers suddenly appeared pushing and shoving and blocking his way.

Just a guard with a whistle.

"Hurry up there!" one of them said. "Get out of the way or we'll miss our train!"

Mo felt himself being pushed back on to the platform. He was stuck in the middle of the group of waiting passengers. Perhaps he'd better chance his luck and go with them, catch the next train that came in. He could see no ticket office, no inspectors, no timetables, just a guard with a whistle.

He looked round at his fellow passengers. Again there were people clothed in cream jackets and trousers. All had numbers on their backs. The smallest children had 3,4,5. The numbers got bigger as did the children and the adults went up to 24. At least Mo didn't see any higher number than 24. Some travellers were dressed in dark blue, and they had numbers too. One or two were dressed in in different colours, all kinds of shades, clothes that Mo was used to seeing on the people back home. One of these was a rather pretty girl. Mo glanced at her number - 17. She looked nice in a white blouse and long flowered skirt. She noticed Mo looking at her. She smiled and said "Hope that train isn't late.

14

I'm looking forward to a nice long day out seeing my friends."

"Where do you have to go?" Mo asked politely.

"Well, I have to take this cake to No. 11 Ogist." (She tapped a cake tin she was holding). "And then I must go back to Plumday."

'Back to Plumday!' thought Mo. He was a bit puzzled.

A gentleman on Mo's other side looked at his watch. So did Mo. 'An odd watch!' he thought.

For there was on the watch something like a needle pointing to the north. On the rim of the watch was a circle, with the hours painted on it. The needle pointed to nine at the top of the watch. As Mo watched there was a little 'tick' and the nine moved the tiniest bit.

A rather pretty girl with a cake tin.

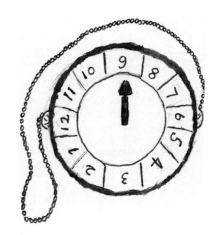

What an odd watch!

Before Mo could wonder further, however, a train drew in to the platform and stopped. It wasn't the kind of train Mo was used to travelling in. The carriages were open, painted blue and gold with skimpy little sunshades that gave little protection from the sun, which was now quite warm.

'But what do they do when it rains?' thought Mo.

"Get wet" said the girl who was No.17, as if he had spoken aloud. "But we're never in the train long anyway."

Mo eased himself into a seat beside No. 17 and asked cautiously "What's Plumday?"

No. 17 looked at Mo, astonished. "Plumday is - well, Plumday. It's Plumday every day for me. His house is always there." She pointed down the street to what seemed empty space. It was a good way off.

"I don't understand" he said.

"You see that street?" said No. 17.

"Yes" said Mo.

"Well, right at the end of it is a square, all the days of the week have houses there. Chatterday, Plumday, Bunday, Cuesday, and so on

All the time. I am 17. My name's Evelinda. I am five o'clock in the after-

It wasn't the kind of train Mo was used to.

noon in Plumday's house. So I've always got to make the tea" she added, by way of more explanation.

"Then it isn't five o'clock yet?" asked Mo, though from the position of the sun he knew it couldn't be.

"Oh no. It's nine o' clock so I've time to deliver this cake and have a day out." Again she patted the cake tin (which she now had on her knee). "It's going to be a lovely day so I shall enjoy my trip. I came to the station from the square walking up Dune which is near to our house. I shall be on this train till Ogist when I will get off, deliver the cake and see my friends at No.11. Then at quarter to five I shall walk right down the rest of Ogist. Then, back to Plumday's house. Where I shall make the tea."

Mo's mind was whirling a bit. 'Where on earth am I?' he wondered.

"That station was Dune" said Evelinda. (Not really the answer to his question).

"And this one we are coming to?" asked Mo.

"Duly, of course."

The streets were like spokes of a wheel

17

Between the stations seemed to be parkland, with deer strolling among the trees. There were open spaces where boys were playing with model aeroplanes.

The train stopped. Mo looked beyond the station. He saw another street, more or less the same as the one he had come from, terrace houses at a right angle to the station, stretching down to no - he couldn't see the square. The gardens of the houses were leafy and full of flowers.

The train moved on, very slowly it seemed to Mo. Then it stopped again.

'I wonder who lives there'

"Here we are!" said Evelinda."Ogist. Bye Bye!"

And she got out of the train, carrying her cake. Mo thought 'Why did she catch the train at all? It would be much quicker surely to walk across the square?'

He peered down the street called Ogist. Another street leading to the square.

'Spokes of a wheel' he said. 'The streets are all like the spokes of a wheel. And the railway line is like the rim of the watch. Or like a clock.'

Mo was so busy thinking he did not notice that the weather was getting dull and the train had stopped several times. People got in and out and now they were all in warmer clothes, sheepskin coats or corduroys, and stout boots. Mo decided to look at the street where the train had stopped. A beautiful, large white painted house in its own grounds stood near the railway station. It had five steps, below which was a basement, to a big oak door, with large windows on either side of it, and a balcony dividing the ground and first floors. Windows pierced the roof.

'I wonder who lives there' thought Mo.

The train moved on again. And stopped again. People moved out of the carriage. "Don't forget to send me a valentine" said one of the girls, a No.14."

'Two years younger than Dorinda' thought Mo. Poor Dorinda! How far away from her he was now!

He told himself he had a job to do! (Though he couldn't for the life of him imagine what the job was!).

'And the next station, whatever it is - I get out!'

----

ooOoo

CHAPTER FOUR

The Larch Tortoise

So the next station saw Mo out of his seat being pushed onto the platform by a crowd of passengers also getting out. He looked at the by now familiar pattern of the streets.

The first house he came to, No.1, however, stood by itself, a cottage with small windows, and a thatched roof, its chimneys at either end. These had funny little heads carved into them on each side of the chimney stacks, little heads that stuck out with a kind of hump where the neck should be. There were daffodils in the garden.

'A good sign' thought Mo. He walked through them by a little white path that led up to a white front door where he knocked, quite sharply.

And then he got the shock of his life!. The door was opened by the Second Footman from the palace back home.

"It's you!" said the Second Footman.

Mo was struck dumb.

The Second Footman turned his head and shouted to someone inside the house "It's that blessed cat!"

And then he walked back into the house.

But the white door was open. Mo waited a moment or two to see if the Footman would appear again. He didn't. So Mo cautiously and quietly went into the house.

What he saw before him was a large kitchen, for all the world like the kitchen back home. There was Ysa the kitchenmaid but she wasn't scrubbing the floor. She was eating bread and butter. The palace cook was there too rolling out pastry.

"Hallo, Mo" she said. "I'm making one of your favourites - meat patties." She gave Mo a patty from a tray that had just been cooked. 'That's odd' thought Mo, 'She always called me Tom!'

Mo nibbled at the patty. Ugh! No proper patty this! It tasted of cardboard. He wondered if it would be impolite to get his sandwiches out of his bag. He decided it would. He ate the patty.

There was a question he wanted to ask.

"How is it that you, and Ysa and the Footman for that matter are, well, here, in this house, in this odd country?"

The door was opened by the Second Footman

"We're dreaming of you. Back home, dreaming" said the cook. We can get here because he - ". She pointed to the only other person in the room - " he tends to wobble a bit."

The other 'person' in the room was a large tortoise, the largest tortoise that Mo had ever seen. He was at least as big as Mo when he was sitting down. The tortoise had a browny blue shell and a very scaly head. His eyes were closed but when the cook talked about 'wobbling' he opened them for an instant, then closed them again.

"You're not dreaming" the cook went on. "I don't know how you got here."

Mo decided not to mention the rocking-horse or Dorinda. The cook was a bit of a gossip.

Instead Mo looked at the tortoise carefully. Wobble? What did she mean? He seems to be just a tortoise, all shell and wrinkles. But what's wrong with his watch?

For the tortoise had a watch in front of him on the floor. As Mo looked at him he opened his eyes again and started to shake the contents of a salt cellar over it, holding the salt cellar with one of his scaly little hands. There was salt over everything, the creature's head, his neck, the floor - everything. Mo drew a little closer and saw that the watch was just the same as the other he had seen - a needle pointing north while a circle moved above it.

With a sigh the tortoise shook the salt again and peered very short-sightedly at the watch, craning his neck as far as it would go.

"It won't work" he said, in a squeaky voice.

"Do you know what's wrong with it?" asked Mo.

Shaking the contents of a salt cellar over it

"Well, you see this arrow pointing to the top of the watch - when the number comes to the top it means that it's time for a new hour. The dial should whizz round once with a whistling noise to let me know the new hour has started. And it won't whizz and it won't whistle. So the number is stuck at the top of

22

the watch. So I'm stuck in here in the kitchen having saucers of tea all day."

Mo could not imagine a tortoise drinking tea at all! But he said politely

"Can't you go out then if your watch doesn't go?"

"No. If my watch doesn't go then I don't go."

A pause.

"Who are you?" asked the tortoise.

"I'm Mo" said Mo. "Who are you?"

"Well, this house is No.1 Larch so I must be the Larch Tortoise."

"Don't you really know?" asked Mo.

"Well, my watch has stopped so everything has gone rather queer. Tell me about yourself and we can change the subject."

Mo thought the tortoise, like the cook, was the sort of person who wouldn't mind a gossip. Dorinda was no business of a tortoise. No, he, Mo, had to be careful whom he told about all Dorinda. So Mo began

"I travelled on the train with a very nice girl. She said she was Evelinda and had to go home to make the tea. At Plumday's" Mo added.

"It's very nice at Plumday's at teatime. I go there myself. When I'm invited" said the tortoise.

"How does one get there?" asked Mo.

"Just walk down the street and you'll come to the square. All the days of the week live there. My favourite is coffee cake" said the tortoise.

Mo understood the coffee cake to be what the tortoise ate for tea - at Plumday's in the square.

"I feel like a bit of coffee cake right now" said the tortoise.

Mo decided he could not help in that.

"There are twelve streets aren't there?"

"Yes" said the tortoise.

23

"And if you walk up a street you come to the station?"

"And if you walk down one you come to the square."

"So in most cases walking across the square would get you to where you wanted to go much more quickly than the train?"

"Yes." The tortoise nodded his scaly head.

"So why are there so many people using the train?" asked Mo.

"Yes, why?" asked the tortoise of himself.

"People get off and on, and still have to walk home" said Mo.

"We like being out of our houses" said the tortoise. "We like the train. We go round and round, round and round, round and round...."

I have a race with that hare down the road

24

Mo wondered how the tortoise moved at all. How could he push through crowds and run along a station platform? But perhaps, thought Mo, he has such a heavy shell it doesn't matter if people bump into him....he just lumbers along....

"I can get along quite fast, you know. Every year I have a race with that hare down the road and I always beat him."

The tortoise's voice seemed to be getting weaker.

Mo peered at him. Yes, he was definitely getting a bit misty around the edges. And his shell seemed to be getting paler - more like beige than brown. He was getting smaller and fatter, and rounder.

Mo thought 'Is he wobbling?'

He heard a laugh, the cook's laugh. He turned round but there was nobody in the kitchen. The rolling pin lay idle, the pastry uncut. Ysa was gone too. Just a shred of bitten crust lay on her plate.

He heard again the voice of the tortoise.

"Just remembered. I'll get toothache."

Mo saw a large coffee cake on the table. The tortoise was nowhere to be seen. The space on the floor where it had been was empty.

'I never saw him jump anywhere' said Mo to himself. 'He is indeed sprightly for a tortoise!'

He saw that the coffee cake was beginning to sprout a few browny scales all round it.

'I'd better go, too' thought Mo, 'before he turns into a tortoise again. He's too wobbly for me.' And he hurried out of the house.

———————

ooOoo

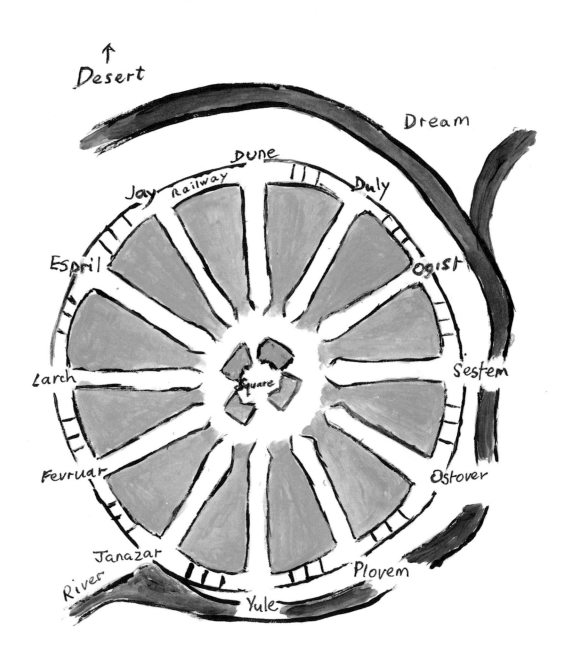

Map of Kalendtown

CHAPTER FIVE

Jay

As he turned into Larch Mo was met by an icy blast of wind. People were scurrying about wrapped in scarves and overcoats and woolly hats. He decided not to walk to Plumday's house. Not in Larch anyway so back he turned back to the station.

'Let's go somewhere warmer!'

When the train stopped again it was warmer. But Mo didn't like the look of the

It was a crazy house

house that faced the station. It was a crazy house such as he had seen at the fair. There was a spiral staircase on the outside going up to a platform with a slide from the platform down to the ground again. Children were going up and down, up and down. A black spiralling path led round the back somewhere. People had to follow the spiral - no walking straight up to a front door - at least none that Mo could see. The windows were set on a slant to one side and on the other side there were no

windows at all. Children were running all round the garden chasing each other with sticks. Two children were playing on a see saw. As it went up and down they tried to hit each other with bags of flour on the end of a rope. They were getting all white and dirty. Two other children were standing up to their knees, fully dressed, in a pond and were splashing water all over each other. Mo thought he would not enjoy doing that at all. Water! Ugh!

The whole scene made Mo feel uneasy. 'Steer clear of that!' he thought. He was a bit wary of children. Some of them seemed to think chasing him and grabbing his tail was fun!

So he stayed on the train a bit longer.

The beautiful girl was not Dorinda after all

And then he saw a most charming villa, a beautiful green lawn and a maypole with ribbons of softly glowing colours, and a beautiful girl picking cherry blossom.

"Dorinda!" he shouted. And he fairly leaped out of the train when it stopped. And ran to the gate of the villa (No.1.again). And saw that the beautiful girl was not Dorinda after all. She just had Dorinda's golden hair. But she smiled at him and waved her sprig of cherry blossom at him.

"Do come in!" she said.

And the gate opened of its own accord.

In Mo walked. The grass felt very soft under his feet. And the flowers gave out a lovely perfume.

"Come and have some lemonade" said the beautiful girl.

She took Mo by the hand and led him to a shady spot beneath a large oak tree in full leaf where more smiling girls were filling glasses on trestle tables covered with white cloths.

Mo fell fast asleep straightaway

"I am Jay" said the beautiful girl.

"I am Mo" said Mo.

Jay took a glass of lemonade and handed it to him. He suddenly felt thirsty. He drank it. It was the best glass of lemonade he had ever tasted.

"We're having a jaypole dance later this morning. But you look tired. Come into the house and have a rest."

She was right, thought Mo. He suddenly did feel very tired. He yawned deeply and allowed Jay to lead him inside her house. He was shown a big room with a floor that shone like glass where green and silver sofas were placed around at gracious angles. He and Jay passed through it. Up some stairs and then a landing and Jay threw open the door of a little room where the wallpaper had a pattern of pink and grey kittens. Mo felt very young again, but why was he so tired? The bed, with its white coverlet looked so inviting!

With a smile Jay was gone. Mo hung his bag from the bedpost and lay down. He fell straightaway fast asleep.

And when he woke up he had forgotten Dorinda and Aunt Daffodil and and the desert and everything else.

---

ooOoo

He would see the sly face of a fairy

CHAPTER SIX

Time goes by

Time was passing as in a dream. Every day Mo woke up in his little white bed to see the sun shining and hear happy laughter outside his window from the dancers on the lawn. He would join them after a lovely breakfast of bacon, toast and marmalade. Strangely he enjoyed seeing the small children moving in a circle round the 'jaypole', (as everyone in the house called it), criss-crossing the ribbons. They didn't try to pull his tail.

Sometimes he jumped to the top of the jaypole and looked down at the dancers below. He got a good view of the whole of the garden. If he turned his head to the right he saw the long hawthorn hedge. He could swear a fox looked out at him from the undergrowth. Turn his head to the left and he would see the sly face of a fairy through the leaves of the oak tree.

He would walk with Jay through the avenues of cherry blossom. Sometimes something would stir in his memory. But then Jay would smile and he would forget what it was.

The afternoons were spent more quietly. Jay read, or played cards, or chess, or gave teaparties. Chess was very strange, Mo thought. Who had played chess with him long ago? With Jay he didn't always win.

The evenings, on the other hand, could be wild. Four sheepdogs would arrive and form a rock band. Bang! would go the drums, the cymbals clash and the beat go boom! boom! boom!. Jay's house would fill with a whirling mass of girls and boys from Mo knew not where. The chatter and laughing and drinking and dancing would go on till dawn. It was quite a relief to Mo to stagger to his bed.

Not all nights were spent in parties. Sometimes no-one came to the house and Mo and Jay sat sipping Jay's cowslip wine and listening to music - strange wild melodies, from flute or violin or guitar, while the moon turned the garden to silver.

Mo switched on the Picturebox

One night was different. Jay said to Mo

"I am starting this evening at an aerobics class."

Aerobics? wondered Mo. And again something stirred. Didn't someone he once knew try aerobics? But gave them up in favour of tobogganing down a mountainside?

Aloud he said "I'll miss you then."

"Oh, you'll be all right" said Jay. "you can watch the Picturebox and I'll leave you a bottle of wine out."

So that evening off she went and Mo switched on the Picturebox. Pictures, flickering shadows, filled the Box. From what Mo could make out they were of elves dancing.

'Wispgel makes your shoes grow lighter,

Wispgel makes your life grow brighter'.

Mo thought this sounded a bit silly. It was the first time he had thought anything at Jay's silly. He could understand anyone wanting comfortable shoes and a brighter life but why such a poor rhyme and jingling tune? And then a voice said 'Try Wispgel on the soles of your shoes and you'll be able to dance till dawn.'

'Oh!' thought Mo. And then 'I wonder if Jay and her friends use Wispgel on their shoes and that's why they can dance without getting tired.' He did not want in the slightest to try Wispgel for himself. Odd! because he enjoyed Jay's parties. He always ended the evening tired out.

Then the picture changed. A little girl in a green cloak was walking through a forest.

'And now we bring you the tale of Little Green Riding-Hat.'

'Little Green Riding-Hat!' Mo's memory stirred . He knew that tale! He had heard it from someone a long, long time ago when he was a kitten. But he thought he would have liked a more modern story now.

Mo switched off the Picturebox. He needed to think. His mind was not working as it had been yesterday.

A drink then to help him concentrate? He got up from the sofa, strode to the sideboard, and opened one of the cupboard doors. He took out a bottle.

'Empty!' he said in disappointment. 'She was so keen to get to aerobics she forgot to leave me one! I'll have to go down to the cellar.'

Mo went downstairs to the kitchens on his way to the cellar. He could hear the maids singing the latest pop tune, not gossiping or laughing or clattering dishes like most maids. Mo thought for the first time that they sounded odd, all singing together, like a choir. He did not want to disturb them and glided swiftly by the kitchen and down the cellar stairs. He opened the cellar door which was not locked. And was just about to pick out a bottle of the best cowslip wine when something else odd caught his eye. It must be his day for oddness, he thought. He had seen an old trunk, such as children took to boarding school, but faded now having seen better days. Trunks are not usually kept in cellars, thought Mo. Trunks are usually kept in attics. Something stirred in Mo's memory again. And this time there was no Jay to smile at him and make him forget. Such a trunk as this as Dorinda had had in her attic 'den'!

Cautiously Mo lifted the lid of the trunk. And he gave a little cry, for looking back at him from the depth of the trunk amid a faded pile of lace and satin was a small doll. Her long hair was untidy, her face full of fine cracks, but her eyes were sharp. It was Dorinda's doll!

"Dorinda!" said Mo. A loud bell seemed to ring in his head.

And then he remembered every thing very clearly. He had to save Dorinda. What was he doing in this strange house, drinking wine, playing about jaypoles? Wasting time! He had to get on, and that meant get out!

Up out of the cellar he rushed - past the kitchens. He was just going through the hall when he remembered again so he turned and ran upstairs into his bedroom. Hastily he grabbed his bag from the bedpost, rushed downstairs again, went out of the door and through the garden. A sheepdog was growling close at hand - he felt the hot breath of something fierce and doglike on the back of his neck! But he got to the gate! As he knew it wouldn't open for him he seized one of the gateposts and swung himself over it. And then he ran and ran even though everything was dark.

ooOoo

CHAPTER SEVEN

The Square

Mo ran till he had a stitch in his side. And lo and behold! he was in the square.

'At last I've found it', he thought 'I must have run all the way down the street from 1 to 31.' Yes - he peered through the darkness and could just make out the number of the last house - No. 31. The night was very dark but there didn't seem to be anyone about - a few people going home from a party at No.30. But nobody seemed to notice Mo.

'I'd better settle down somewhere for the night.' And he thought of his little white bed at Jay's with just a little bit of sadness. 'It will have to be a park bench tonight' he sighed.

Mo found a bench in one of the small parks which were around the square and sat down on it. He got to thinking about the strangeness of the evening. How had Dorinda's trunk come to be in the cellar? Who had put the idea of aerobics in Jay's head, and switched her full bottle for the empty one?

Thinking about this Mo fell asleep.

The new day dawned. Mo woke up to the sound of someone coughing. A cleaning lady was sweeping the path outside No.31 and the dust was getting to her. Mo woke up and opened his eyes and remembered the night before. A horrid thought struck him. He looked down to see if he still had his bag. Oh, yes, he found that he had.

'If I had left it Jay would have been able to get me back to her.' This was such a

It was Dorinda's Doll

disagreeable thought to Mo now he tried to switch his mind to something else. 'I wonder which is Plumday's house.'

But he wasn't going to knock on any doors for the moment in case he got trapped in another house he couldn't get out of.

He wondered if his sandwiches were still in the bag. They were, and as he was feeling quite hungry by this time, he started to eat them. Surprisingly they were still quite fresh and tasty.

Mo looked again at the square. It seemed to have parkland at each corner of it, for there were fine trees, play areas for children and places for people to walk their dogs. Four roads led from it to a circular road from which twelve streets spread out like the spokes of a wheel. A flowerbed circular in shape was exactly in the middle of it, full of orange flowers. Seven houses stood in the square. Three sets of streets had two and one set had only one.

'I bet that's Plumday's' thought Mo, but he'd had enough of houses for the time being.

He heard a door open and close. And then a familiar form stepped along the path from Plumday's house. It was Evelinda. She had a little white dog on a lead. She was wearing a red anorak and pale pink trousers but she still had a 17 on her back.

Mo said politely "Good Morning."

Evelinda stopped and turned towards him.

"Oh, hello. It's you again. How are you getting on?"

Mo didn't want to tell her about his stay at Jay's, so he said "Oh, not too bad. But I don't really know what I should do next." He paused. "I'm really looking for a bit of advice. It's so confusing in this place."

Evelinda frowned - she didn't like the sound of "this place."

"It's not confusing at all" she said.

"I find things confusing" said Mo. "For instance people travel by train when it would be quicker for them to walk."

"That depends on where you're going. Travel from No.1 Ogist to No.1

Fevruar, for instance, and the train is quicker. The train is quicker all the time. When we're on it we only have to blink our eyes and we're where we want to be."

Mo wondered if that meant passengers fell asleep and ran the risk of missing their station.

Evelinda went on. "You argue too much" she said.

Mo hadn't thought he was arguing. But Evelinda started to walk away from him. "Come on, Fido" she said to the dog.

Mo felt a great disappointment. Evelinda stopped. She turned her head and said "Janus. See Janus." And then she turned a corner and was out of sight.

---

ooOoo

A draft of very cold air caught him as he sat in the park

CHAPTER EIGHT

Janus

After Evelinda had gone Mo thought 'Who's Janus?' He strolled over to his park bench again, his mind busy. The morning sun was pleasant on his fur.

'Janus. Where does Janus live?'. Mo thought of all the strange names he had seen. He must be something to do with a month, like Larch - March, May - Jay. 'Here all the names get twisted into something else. What would his number be?'

Mo remembered a Roman called Janus, with two heads, one to look forward, one to look back. Two heads are better than one. 'The owner gets a double dose of wisdom' he supposed. But he thought he didn't want to meet anyone with two heads. He'd met quite enough odd people, thank you.

A drift of very cold air caught him as he sat in the park. Strange, it had been warm and sunny only a moment ago. Mo left his bench and walked across the square. The cold air was coming from one of the streets. Mo tried to see the name of it, almost covered in snow.

"Janazar" he said. The number of the house nearest him was 31. What was Janus' number?

Mo thought the best thing to do would be to walk along the street and find a house big enough for such an important person. Who was important at home in Janazar?

The answer was not long in coming to him, for there was only one important day that he could think of. 'New Year's Day, of course!' thought Mo, triumphantly. 'No. 1!'

He set off on his walk. Janazar was a quiet street. It was very cold with very few people out and about, only more cleaning ladies sweeping snow away from front doorsteps.

Mo went quickly along the street right to the top of it to the gate of No.1 and found to his pleasant surprise that Janus lived in the beautiful big house he had first seen from the train, the one with the oak door, the large windows and the balcony.

He pushed open the gate.

'How lucky he is to have all those snowdrops out' thought Mo.

His paws tapped on the icy path and he climbed the steps carefully to the front door. The knocker was higher up than he could reach but the door opened and a tall manservant, dressed all in black, said "Come in, sir. You are expected."

And Mo walked into a hall of such size it reminded him of the one in the palace at home. There were ancestors enough hanging in portraits on the walls to remind him of his own proud family. "But they were cats" he thought "and these are not."

Mo drew himself up to his full height.

"I have come to see Mr.Janus" he said.

"Sir Janus will see you in a moment. Meanwhile sit down and make yourself comfortable." And the manservant, who was a butler, went away.

Mo sat down in a gold chair with red velvet cushions which was at the end of a long marble table on which a gold set of candlesticks sparkled, the lights of the candles reflected on the table's polished top.

Mo sat down on a gold chair

Suddenly there was the rustle of a long curtain covering a doorway and a very old gentleman in a black suit and a grey, curled wig, with a lacy shirt front tumbling in front of his waistcoat, stood before him.

Mo leaped to his feet and gave a very low bow.

"Sir" he said.

The old gentleman raised his hand.

39

A very old gentleman stood before him

"There is no need for you to explain. I know all. I have watched your progress on my computer screen. You are sent to help Dorinda here in Kalendtown."

'Kalendtown?' thought Mo. 'Well, at least there is someone here who knows about Dorinda.'

"Do you remember the desert?" asked Janus.

"Yes" said Mo.

"The desert is made of the sands of time" Janus went on. "The sands swirl and change. So do the clouds. Nothing stays the same for long. You saw the castle - that is Timeago. It is not real any more, it is all the past."

"Then it was a good thing I didn't go there" said Mo.

"Indeed. It would have been a complete waste of time. Or the vultures would have won."

Mo's thoughts on this kept him silent.

Janus sat down in a chair at the other end of the table.

"And, young man, You see I do not have two heads. One head is quite enough for anybody. But", he added as an afterthought, "I do need my computer."

Mo felt a bit uncomfortable for thinking that Janus might have two heads.

"So this is Kalendtown?" he said.

"Yes" said Janus. "You will have observed that all the streets in this town stand for one month of the year, each house being one day of the month, where 24 hours live. So there are the dark blue night hours, while the ones in cream are day hours. The hours that belong to the Special Days can wear what they like."

"Well," said Mo. "At home the hours pass one after another all going forward. They're not people, talking and walking about."

"Ah, at home things are a bit different. Here we are all days and hours moving about as we please, more or less. Days have numbered hours, but when these have done their special work they are free of time. My cook watches the Picturebox all day as well as thinking of all the meals and getting them ready on time. My butler cleans the silver or orders the groceries, or does the accounts. Then he goes to the races.

All my servants have lots of parties. I watch time and all the changes it brings, on my screen."

"So that's why Evelinda thinks about teatime! And you, Sir Janus, are a Special Day so your tasks are different. Just as Jay's were different."

"Jay's work is all play and spring magic" said Janus.

"Will Evelinda make the tea for ever?" asked Mo. "Do the hours always stay the same age?"

"Every year everybody moves up one and one new baby is born. 2 becomes 3, 3 becomes 4, and so on. All the hours have a birthday on the same day and change their numbers. Next year Evelinda will be 18, six o'clock, which is the hour for bathing the baby."

"What happens to 24?" asked Mo. he had see nobody above 24. "Do they die?"

"They move on to another part of the universe and start again. Time goes on everywhere you know," said Janus. "They don't die, at least not here. The Special Days, on the other hand, don't move. They, myself included, are all 24s who have been here for hundreds of years, since your Calendar was made."

"And Jay?" asked Mo.

"As old as the rest of us" said Janus.

"Do people sleep at night? Do day hours not sleep at all?"

"Oh, people sleep when they feel tired. As long as they do the tasks of their hour. The very youngest hours sleep when they want, as they have always done everywhere."

"And the days of the week?" asked Mo.

"The Days of the week are a bit different" replied Janus. "Six Days run shops."

Mo considered this. He had never thought he might go shopping in this odd country. Come to think of it, though, Jay must have done a lot of shopping to keep her larder as full as she had. But he himself had no money to go shopping with.

"Never mind, Mo. You have no time to go shopping" said Janus as though he could read his thoughts. "Your task is with Dorinda."

Mo had an idea. "Do you think I should find Dorinda's birthday in one of the streets round here?"

"No, the hours will be going about their own business as usual. They know Dorinda fell asleep and wrote all about it in a book. That's as much as they'll do. You must find not Dorinda's birthday, but her dream, her great idea."

"Her great idea?" Mo asked, wonderingly.

"Yes. Ideas, plans, dreams - they're all here too but outside the town, along the river bank."

"She wanted a swimming-pool" said Mo. "That was the idea in her mind round about her birthday."

"Then look for a swimming-pool" said Janus "I will lend you my boat for your trip down the river."

Janus rose. So did Mo. Janus rang the bell and his butler appeared.

"Take this young gentleman to the boat". And to Mo "Farewell, young fellow. Take care. The Espril Fool is always on the look out for people to play his tricks on. And don't go near No. 31 Ostover."

The butler led Mo out of the room, down dark passages through a tunnel running from the back of the house, out into the daylight. Mo was on some steps going down to the bank of a river and a little boat was moored at the side of them.

Mo hated water, but he went down the steps and got into the boat. It pushed away from the steps by itself and slowly started to drift downstream, into the region of Dream.

———————

ooOoo

CHAPTER NINE

The Summerhouse

The scene on the river bank was different again from any thing Mo had seen in the town. People were busy working on all kinds of things. He passed men building what looked to be a cathedral, then a dockyard where lay a huge ship. Then a hangar with the nose of a rocket pointing out, then a row of little bungalows and cottages with roses round the door. People were playing cricket - Mo heard the roar of a football crowd from a big stadium.

Then he saw the shops. Big department stores. They all looked the same from the windows, exactly the same goods were on show in each - ski suits, blue and cream clothes, swimming costumes, anoraks, dresses of all colours- all were the same. "Department Store" was printed above the window of each one, but the first was 'Bunday', No. 2 'Cuesday'. No. 3 'Medmesday' right up to No. 6 'Chatterday'. Mo could see as he sailed by people going in and out of the shop No. 2 'Cuesday'. Food and furniture seemed to be on the ground floor, ladies' hats on the first floor and a restaurant with people dining on the second floor. The queer thing was only Cuesday was open. The rest of the shops were closed.

A little boat was moored

'So it's Cuesday today' thought Mo.

The boat drifted on down the river. Mo saw a few trees on the river bank, then an open field. He had left the town far behind by now.

The boat stopped by a paved court in which were planted little rose bushes. Mo remembered that Dorinda was going to dig up the roses in her garden (Horrible thought!) so she could have a swimming-pool in their place. But here was a swimming-pool as well as the roses! And at the side of the pool there was a little summerhouse. It looked like Dorinda's summerhouse.

Mo jumped out of the boat, ran along the path and ran to the door, bursting it open. And what did he see? No less than Dorinda's attic, her playroom. There was a rocking-horse, a box of jewels, and the dollshouse was there, and Dorinda's jigsaws and a whole heap of old toys.

Mo looked carefully at the rocking-horse. Was it his rocking-horse? He reached out a paw and touched its nose.

The horse neighed angrily and it all turned black. Mo was a bit scared by it. Definitely not my rocking-horse, he thought. But oh where oh where was the horse he had lost?

Mo looked afresh at the room. Yes, there was something else, something that had once been in the cupboard. On the windowsill was a brightly coloured round object, a bit like a paperweight. Mo picked it up. It was a globe on its own small stand. Its entire surface was made of twenty five six-sided pieces, red, blue, orange, green and yellow. The coloured pieces were all mixed up all over the globe.

'It's a puzzle - a puzzle called a Zebek globe', thought Mo. 'I remember Dorinda had a globe like this.'

He looked again at the rocking-horse (not black any more) and at all the toys and objects in the room. They were all as he remembered them at home. Now they were all here in Dream. What was he do do next?

Suddenly it came into his mind that solving the puzzle was very very important. You had to get all the pieces of the same colour together so the globe looked one bit all red, one bit all blue, and so on.

On the windowsill was a brightly coloured round object

So Mo twisted the sides of the globe for the pieces all moved up and down and sideways. He twisted them again and again. At least half an hour went by. No matter how he twisted and turned the pieces the colours never got to their proper sides all together. At times it seemed as if he had almost got it right, but the the globe would twist of its own accord and the pieces were all mixed up again.

'I'll have to take it back to Janus' thought Mo.

So he put the globe in his little bag (empty of sandwiches now) and made his way to the boat again. The current of the river seemed to have changed. The boat should have had a harder time going upstream, making the return journey, but it drifted along pleasantly as before. It moored itself at Janus' steps. Mo got out of it to enter the tunnel that led back to Janus' house. The change from light to dark was very sudden. Mo found he couldn't see for a moment.

He felt something coming down over his head. His wrists were forced behind his back and handcuffs were put on them.

And a voice said "Gotcha! Espril Fool!".

---

ooOoo

CHAPTER TEN

Espril Fool

Mo was led by his captors out of the tunnel.

They all travelled along for quite a way. He thought he must be in a park area close to Janazar station. Where were they going?

Hee-Haw! Hee-Haw! And the sound of hooves. There must be at least three men here, thought Mo. And a donkey? Then he nearly had the breath knocked out of him as he was roughly flung on the back of one. Someone climbed up behind him and a voice said "Gee up!".

Mo would remember that ride for ever. Bumped and banged so that every bone in his his body ached, with the man behind him breathing on his neck. And the laughing. His captors had done nothing but laugh ever since they had caught him as though it was a great joke to catch someone, and handcuff him, then throw him on the back of a donkey like a sack of onions. Mo hoped there would be a passerby who would come to his aid but there was no-one. Anyway the people of this town were quite used to seeing Espril Fool and his friends taking prisoners. So no-one stopped the men and their donkey.

Just as Mo was beginning to think he could stand things no longer he was pulled from the donkey's back and the covering on his head was whipped off. He was able to see the men who had caught him. They were - three clowns in striped baggy clown suits with bobbles on their shoes, and on their hats. One was in a red and white striped suit with red bobbles on his hat and shoes, and he had a clown's red nose and white face. He also wore a bright red wig. The second clown had a red nose and a white face but he was in green and white stripes and wore a green wig. The third clown had a white face, a red nose and a silver striped suit. He was wearing a white wig. Red wig blew a squeaker in Mo's face. Green wig tweaked his ear. This was really too much! Mo gave a tiny hiss.

The clowns nearly fell over laughing.

"Into the house with you!" said red wig. The other two grabbed Mo by the arms and started to march him along the crazy black path that went round and round in a spiral before it reached - yes, the door of the crazy house Mo had seen earlier from the train, the crazy house with the slide going down from the roof, and the slanted windows that gave the house a funny lopsided look.

Mo was marched round the windowless side to the back where the strange slanting door was standing open.

"Into the house with you" said red wig again and he gave Mo a push. As he went through the door a bag of flour fell from it, missing him by inches. The clowns laughed and laughed. Mo thought they couldn't have laughed more if the bag of flour had hit him.

A custard pie flew through the air and hit one of the clowns in the face. He wiped the bits from his eyes and laughed till the tears started in them.

A bag of flour fell

Mo felt what seemed like a banana skin under his foot and he managed to not step on it. Green wig did step on it. He fell and started laughing just like a donkey. Hee-Haw! Hee-Haw!.

The room in which they were now in had a black plastic floor and pink, shocking pink, walls. It was absolutely bare.

"I'm Alonso" said red wig. And he gave Mo a low bow. "That's Beppo." He pointed to green wig. "And he is Grindo." He nodded towards white wig. And then he started turning cartwheels all over the room non-stop.

"I suppose that's why there's no furniture" thought Mo.

There stood a man in jester's costume

He found it a relief that the clowns didn't seem to want to know who he was or ask any questions.

Beppo produced three coloured balls, green, red and white, out of the air and started to juggle with them. Grindo stopped laughing and began to cry instead.

"Boo-hoo! Boo-hoo! he went.

Mo thought "What's he got to cry about? It's me who should be crying!" (Not that he would, in front of them).

There is no telling how long this state of affairs would have gone on - the juggling, the cartwheels and the crying, with Mo standing in the middle of the floor still with his handcuffs on. In fact the clowns seemed to have forgotten he was there at all. When suddenly - Bang! There was the noise of a trapdoor snapping open, a puff of smoke and there stood a man in a jester's costume, green and gold with a spiky stuffed hat covered in little bells . There were bells round his ankles and wrists.

"Espril Fool!" he said. The three clowns stopped everything they were doing. Beppo stopped juggling, Alonso stopped doing cartwheels, and Grindo stopped crying.

The strange man came over to Mo, stood a few feet in front of him and said "Sir. I'm Espril Fool, not at your service!"

Mo just said nothing.

The Fool held out his hand. A white dove flew out of it away up to the rafters. In the other hand he produced a bunch of paper flowers. Then he strolled over to Mo and took a boiled egg out of his ear, and then walked round and took a gold coin out of his other ear.

"Now let's see what you can do! Can you get a boiled egg from my ear?"

"No" said Mo. "Your hat covers your ears."

The Fool laughed.

Then he leaned forward with a serious expression on his face, and asked "But what can you do?"

Mo drew himself up to his full height, nodded towards Beppo and said "I can juggle."

"Give him the balls, Beppo!" said the Fool.

"I can't juggle with handcuffs on" Mo pointed out.

"I'll take them off myself" said the Fool. And he produced from his sleeve a little key, and unlocked Mo's handcuffs.

Mo rubbed his wrists for a minute. His paws were a bit stiff. He put his bag on the floor. Then he took the balls from Beppo.

One, two, three and then the balls were in the air and Mo was juggling splendidly. He had often juggled for Dorinda and could keep going for ages without dropping any balls.

He was juggling only for about a minute and then the Fool seemed to grow tired. He clapped his hands "Stop! Stop!" he ordered.

"Now what about an Oirish jig!" he produced a fiddle from somewhere, handed it to Grindo and said "Play!"

The balls were in the air

So Grindo played and Mo jigged. He folded his arms, and his little feet leaped and twinkled and criss-crossed in mid-air, he twirled and whirled, and jigged for all he was worth.

The Fool clapped his hands again and said "Enough!" Then he said slyly "Can you play the fiddle while we jig?"

Mo had never touched a fiddle in his life, let alone played one, but he took the fiddle from the Fool, and drew the bow across the strings. The bow seemed to take on a life of its own. Back and forth across the strings it went in the merriest tune Mo had ever heard, though he knew he had no control of it. The Fool and the clowns all began to jig and somersault and turn cartwheels all over the room.

The bow seemed to take on a life of its own

After about a minute the Fool collapsed in a heap on the floor. So did the three clowns.

"Refreshment is called for" said the Fool. He got to his feet and beckoned to Mo. "Come into the garden." And he strolled to the window and climbed out. So did the three clowns. Mo thought he'd better follow so, picking up his bag, he climbed out of the window too.

The window gave out onto the lawn and Mo could survey the scene. It hadn't changed from last time. Children were still climbing up to the roof and following one another down the slide. The two on the see saw were still hitting each other with bags of flour, and the two children in the duckpond were still splashing about.

The Fool signalled to Mo to walk with him across the lawn to a big tent. There was an ice cream kiosk on the way halfway across the lawn.

"Have an ice lolly" said the Fool. And he picked out a raspberry ice lolly and gave it to Mo.

Mo was glad. He felt a bit thirsty after all that jigging. But when he tried to lick it he found it was made of plastic. He threw it in a bush when the Fool and the clowns weren't looking.

They all got to the tent. Mo looked hard at the food. The salmon sandwiches were made of cardboard, the rock cakes were real rock, and the meringues were plaster of Paris.

"Try a jam tart" said the Fool. But the jam tarts were no better. They were some kind of soft paste, like putty.

"Try a jam tart"

But then the Fool's attention was taken by two children, in very wet clothes, running to him.

"Can we have him? Can we have him?" pointing to Mo.

"What for?" said the Fool.

"For the pond!" said one of the children "We're getting a bit tired of just splashing us!"

"Sure, take him away!" said the Fool, throwing up his arms as though he was being very generous.

So again Mo found himself being marched away, this time, to the pond.

They got to the edge.

"Now you take his left paw" said one of the children, "and I'll take his right."

Mo couldn't hiss, he couldn't growl. Only a soft gurgle came out of his throat. This was awful!

He was led right to the edge of the pond. Then suddenly, just as he expected to be thrown into the water with a great splash, there was an ear-piercing blast! Mo thought it was his own voice screeching but then realised the sound came from a young girl blowing a whistle from the top of the tower where the slide was. She was standing on the platform looking out to the people in the garden, and a big silver whistle at her neck was glistening in the sun.

Without a word the two children took their hands off Mo's paws and started to walk towards the house. Everyone else was walking towards the house. The two children on the see saw climbed off it and walked towards the house. The slide and the ladder to it was empty. The Fool and his clowns made their way towards the house.

Mo looked to the young girl. She turned round to go in the house herself. There was a 12 on her back.

'Of course!' thought Mo. 'Now I understand! Espril Fool must always finish his tricks by 12 o'clock!'

He wondered what they all did the rest of the day, when they were 'free of time.'

He himself turned, not towards the house, but towards the gate! Nobody stopped him. Nobody seemed to notice. He got to the gate just as it was about to lock itself and squeezed through it.

He decided to walk as quickly as possible through Espril and go down to the square again. The sun was warm. He would have a little sleep and try to find a cafe somewhere.

All was quiet in the square, only a washerwoman outside her house pinning clothes on her washline.

'I bet that's Bunday' thought Mo.

He found his park bench, sat down and after a while dozed off. That jig had been very tiring and the pond an awful shock.

++++++++

By the time Mo woke up the sun had set and the darkness had fallen.

'Now for the cafe. But where is it?'

Mo had never actually seen a cafe in the square but he was sure there must be one. All squares had a cafe. So he wandered all round the square. He had no money to pay for food, but he could always offer to help to wash up.

So busy was Mo looking for a cafe that he missed his bearings a bit and turned a corner into a strange street. He had turned into Ostover. Right by No.31.

---

ooOoo

CHAPTER ELEVEN

31 Ostover

"Well, hello there!" said a voice. It was quite a friendly, drawling voice.

"Lovely evening, isn't it?" said another, a bit lighter in tone.

Mo looked about him.

Leaning on a lamppost was a large black cat, its eyes glowing amber. It was much bigger than Mo. At the gate of No.31 was another black cat, also much bigger than Mo.

"Come and join the party" said Cat No.2. And he took Mo's arm, in a friendly fashion.

"Let's all go in together" said Cat No. 1, and he took Mo's other arm, and all three went into No 31's garden where indeed a party was going on.

"We're Halloze'en" said Cat No. 1.

Janus had warned him! Not to go near 31 Ostover! Oh dear, oh, dear!

Every window of the house was lit with a turnip lantern, each candle glowing brightly and shedding an orange light on the scene below. The garden was also lit by more turnip lanterns. Under one of them three small blue hours in pointy hats were sitting. They appeared to be eating pumpkin pie with little forks, or ice cream. 'It must be hard to eat ice cream with a fork' thought Mo.

At the far end of the garden grown up people also in pointy hats were gathered round a bonfire over which a cauldron was hanging. Something was bubbling in the cauldron and every now and then one of the witches (for they were all witches or wizards) would put in a long spoon and fill a mug for one of the other witches. They were all singing strange songs. Mo could hear the tune of 'Ellie Dinne' and 'The Indian sob shriek.'

Mo was being led by the two cats towards this group. But then one of them stopped.

"I've just had the most super idea" he said.

"What?" asked the other.

"Let's play football. Let's have a penalty shoot-out. He" indicating Mo " can be in goal and we two can kick the penalties. The best of six, each. If I win he" indicating Mo again " can work in the office with me. And if you win he can work on the car with you."

"And if it's a draw?"

"He can be in the office and on the car as well."

Both cats seemed to think the penalty shoot-out was a good idea. They found two hawthorn bushes not too far apart and a football.

Something was bubbling in the cauldron

"Right. Ready to start."

Cat No. 1 kicked the ball so fast Mo hardly saw it. Of course it went between the hawthorn bushes.

The second ball was the same.

A young blonde witch walked over from the group of witches and began to watch the game. The two cats stopped playing.

The young witch said "Carry on, boys. But remember I'm in this now."

Mo took a look at her.

'She's just like Dorinda'

A young blonde witch began to watch the game

he thought. Then he pulled his thoughts together, remembering he had considered Jay to be like Dorinda.

And missed penalty No.3.

The next ball, however, was a a bit better. It came towards the hawthorn bush and then seemed just to settle by it.

Ball No.5 dropped right at Mo's feet so he gave it a good kick and it was away.

Ball No. 6 came at his chest. He put out a paw. He hit it easily and again the ball was away.

That was the end of the first cat's game.

"Three-three" said the young witch.

The second cat took his place. The young witch was watching closely.

The second cat's game was pretty much the same as the first's. The ball got between the bushes three times. The other times it either went over the top of the bushes or Mo hit it.So the second cat scored three-three.

"It's a draw! He belongs to both of us!" said the cats delightedly.

The young witch stepped forward. "Hold it, sonnies! Three-three each isn't good enough. Equal means he has a chance to get away from you."

She beckoned to Mo. "Come on out of that goal. Game's over. You're coming with me."

The two cats looked a bit annoyed but they said nothing.

"From now on" said the witch to Mo "you work for me, not them. What's that bag you're carrying? Take it off!".

Mo did not want to do as she said. She held out her hand, the two cats growled. Mo decided he would be safer if he took off the bag containing the precious globe and so he gave it to the witch.

She opened the bag, inspected the globe and said "I like puzzles."

And she twisted and turned the sides of the globe but try as she might she couldn't get the colours to match.

"Let's play another game" she said. And she took Mo's paw and led him to a trestle table standing in a corner of the garden. She placed the globe on it. On the ground underneath the table were three pointy hats. The witch picked them up and placed them in a line on the table, one over the globe.

"Now you tell me which hat the globe is under and you can have it back!"

"That one!" said Mo, pointing to the middle hat.

The witch lifted the hat. No globe.

"That one!" said Mo, pointing to the hat on his right.

The witch lifted the hat. No globe.

"That one!" said Mo, pointing to the hat he had chosen first.

Still no globe.

The witch clapped her hands. "I've won! The globe is mine forever. And you are my servant!"

Then she said, more kindly "You look a bit peaky. Come and have some supper."

She took Mo to a wonderful old machine where an old man was cooking baked potatoes.

"Give him one" she said. "And put plenty of butter on it!"

Mo was glad to get some supper. He was very hungry, and the baked potato tasted really good. No cardboard here!

Three pointy hats

61

When he had eaten it the witch said "We could go ducking for apples.... Or shall we have a nice conversation?". She sat on the ground and patted it for Mo to sit beside her.

"I'm Zanzi, by the way. Who are you?"

"I'm Mo" said Mo. And he told Zanzi all about Jay and about the Espril Fool but not a word about Janus, not a word about Dorinda.

"Jay's a witch, really" said Zanzi "and the Fool is a bit tricksy. But" she leaned closer to Mo, "I've got you now!"

Then she suddenly leaped to her feet. "In the morning you start work!"

Then the two of them went into the house. Mo found himself in a big uncarpeted hall at the end of which was a very imposing staircase. The staircase led to a landing where the stairs split in two, going right and left. There was a large stained glass window on the landing. The picture in it was that of a witch in black robes riding her broomstick, her pale hair flying behind her, all against a background of stars.

Zanzi took the right-hand stair. They got to another landing on which was some very cheap matting. Zanzi pointed to a door.

"That's my bedroom. You sleep on the landing out here."

Mo looked at the matting. It didn't seem very comfortable. Not a bit like Jay's little white bed. He sighed.

Zanzi went into her room and shut the door. Then she opened it again and popped her head out.

"I have my tea at 8 o'clock sharp. Good night!"

The stained glass window

ooOoo

62

CHAPTER TWELVE

Life at No. 31

Mo awoke to the sun's rays streaming in through the windows in the wall by the landing. He heard the sound of feet downstairs.

'Zanzi's tea! I'd better get it or she might turn me into a frog!'

He soon found out where the kitchen was. He just followed the noise where teacups were clattering. Suddenly the kitchen door opened and a chimpanzee carrying a laden tray came rushing out.

A witch in a hat was filling teapots

Mo went in through the door. A witch in a hat and a white cook's apron was filling teapots, rather carelessly, thought Mo, for she was just swinging her arm and letting the water splash into several teapots one after the other. What a strange way to make tea, thought Mo.

"Zanzi's is at the end of the table" said the cook witch. "Look sharp now!"

Mo grabbed the tray at the end of the table with its cup and saucer, milk, sugar and teapot, all swimming in water as it was, and left the kitchen to make his way to Zanzi's bedroom.

"Come in!" said a voice when he knocked on the door. Mo went in.

Zanzi was sitting up in bed (a nice comfortable bed) her hair in a golden cloud spread out over her shoulders.

"Clever Mo! Right on time!"

Mo wasn't listening. He was too busy looking round the room. He saw a large china cabinet, with glass at each side, and at the front of it, including the door, that held all kinds of objects. There were shells of all colours and description, small, big, curled, fan-like; there were tiny dolls and teddies, none of them more than sixteen centimetres high, there were tiny teapots, tiny bowls of glass fruit, little boxes with scenes on them. On the top shelf of the cabinet in the right hand corner was his Zebek globe.

"Locked" said Zanzi, with satisfaction. "And the glass is special so you can't break it."

Mo said nothing. But he thought he would try anything to get his globe back.

Zanzi got out of bed, tweaked Mo's ear, and declared she was going to go for a shower. Mo must wait until she came back.

While Mo waited he looked at his Zebek globe. He examined the lock on the door of the cabinet. It looked as if a very small key would open it. Where did Zanzi keep her keys? In her pockets? In a purse? He opened Zanzi's wardrobe door. Her hat and robes were hanging there. And at the back of the door there was a rack of keys, large keys, medium-sized keys, copper keys, black keys, but none that looked small enough to open the cabinet door. But ah, he'd missed one. There was a small key, right enough!

Zanzi was coming back! Mo stepped out of the wardrobe and shut the door.

She was wearing a dress of some black cottony stuff. She looked rather nice, Mo thought. She had a long necklace of what could have been coffee beans round her neck. On her back was a No.18.

"You'll never manage it!" she said. And she laughed.

Mo stared hard again at the lock. He noticed that there was something odd about the keyhole. It was either made of wood or plastic, or some magic material. It wasn't a metal keyhole. And it seemed to be blocked. Not a real keyhole at all. Blocked by Zanzi's magic.

"You'll never manage it" she said

"Now you can dry my hair" said Zanzi.

So Mo had to dry Zanzi's hair with a hair dryer.

"A lady's maid now, am I?" He wasn't very pleased.

But he found on the whole that working for Zanzi wasn't bad. He shared his meals with her, sitting beside her while she loaded a little plate for him. And the food was good! The cereals really were very tasty, the breakfast bacon was done to a turn, and then there was fresh crisp toast with a delicious marmalade. Just the kind of breakfast that Mo liked!

The two big black cats would often be there too at the table. They worked for all the people at No.31, Mo found out. One of them saw to the bills and other papers and the other was a chauffeur for the witches. He drove their big car for them. (The witches usually travelled on broomsticks but when they needed to dress in ordinary clothes or when it was raining they would travel in their car).

The two cats seemed a bit afraid of Zanzi, who probably could have turned them into frogs if they had been at all impolite.

'Being a lady's maid is probably better than working for those two' thought Mo.

After breakfast Zanzi took Mo to her classroom where she was a teacher. Her pupils were three of the small hours, nos. 4, 5, and 6. They were dressed in blue clothes. Mo thought they were very sweet.

They sat in desks in a row. When Zanzi came in the room they stood up and said "Good Morning, Zanzi."

Zanzi said "Good Morning, children" and told Mo to give the books out.

"Today we start a new book" said Zanzi.

Mo took a glance at the title and saw the book was called 'First Steps in Spells.'

"Open your books at Lesson One. How to turn bubbles into balloons" said Zanzi.

She went to a cupboard by the teacher's desk and got out three sets of rings for blowing and three bowls. One by one the children filled the bowls with water at the sink in the corner of the classroom. Zanzi gave each of the children a packet of magic powder which they all stirred in the water and soon dozens of bubbles were being blown across the room.

The children found turning the bubbles into balloons a bit difficult. They all came out white balloons at first which then had to be changed into coloured ones. Learning how to do this took the children a long time. But by the end of the lesson they had all managed to do it, proceeding from pale pink balloons to red and even one or two blue ones. It was very difficult to make blue ones.

"Tomorrow we'll try making green ones" said Zanzi.

Mo was able to take a look at the book while the children were working. Lesson 2 was about how to turn leaves into writing paper. Lesson 3 how to turn Hlasticine into bars of soap. All very useful!

++++++++

Zanzi did not teach in the afternoons. She went to the printing room where she printed all kinds of notices such as 'Party tonight! Bring your own eats!' 'Dogs must not walk on the grass.' She played about with a big printing press and printed little books. She knew all the ways of printing from start to finish. Her ambition was to print her own book of spells, spells that she herself had invented.

There were classes too; carpentry, furniture making, weaving, sewing, a variety of painting classes and jewellery making classes; there was a class of Ninoese magic and flower painting combined that was very interesting. You held a paintbrush, muttered a few magic words and the paintbrush would go over the paper painting a beautiful flower, all in great detail, while leaving a lot of the paper blank, in the Ninoese way.

There was one witch, called Elor, who was a real whizz at the flower painting. She did it herself without the magic words. That was because she couldn't remember or even say them properly. She had her own particular paintbrush and Mo used to like to watch her paint with it. She was so good at painting and so bad with magic he wondered if the paintbrush had the magic itself. Where had she got it from? With this paintbrush Elor was marvellous at flowers, but she was hopeless with other work. Her turnip lanterns came out cross-eyed and her knitted scarves were more like fishing-nets. As for magic she couldn't do any of it. Her friends despaired of her.

Zanzi did not always work in the afternoons. She had two friends, Melda and Drine. She often used to go out with them. The three of them often joined a group of witches and they all went out together. Witches like going out in groups as they can get more done. When a witch wanted to go out she would open a window, stand on the windowsill and say "Come, broomstick, come!" And a broomstick would come to the window, the witch would climb on it and away she would fly.

Zanzi and her friends would fly away on their broomsticks usually to the Dream part of the country for an afternoon at the races, or to watch football or cricket. Mo would go with them, riding behind Zanzi on the broomstick. He liked seeing the horses racing but he was glad to be at a safe distance from them. They were so big! (It was when he was at the races that he wondered again where his rocking-horse was).

Zanzi and the witches sang loud songs at the football matches, and waved big rattles. The crowd in the stadium never realised they were truly witches, because everybody got dressed up in funny costumes anyway.

It was the same at the cricket matches. But if they thought the game was too slow the witches would make the ball career all over the field, just for fun. And the batsmen would be declared out when they were really not out at all.

Sometimes Zanzi and her friends wanted to play tennis. Then they were a bit naughty. They would swoop down on anyone who was already playing on the tennis court and chase them off it, and then they would take the courts over for hours.

Scarves were more like fishing nets

They were even worse when they went shopping. Zanzi, Melda and Drine would go into Cuesday's (or whichever shop happened to be open) and try all the hats on. They didn't want to buy any hats but just wanted to spend time changing them. If a feather was on a hat when a witch tried it on it would have a flower on it when she took it off. A flower on a hat would be changed into a bunch of grapes. Ribbons would disappear entirely, and brims would change from broad to narrow, or from floppy to curled. Or the other way around.

It was the same with shoes. Buckles and straps would change places and heels would go up or down.

The shop assistants would get very cross but they did not dare tell the witches not to come in the shop again.

+++++++++

In the evenings there were parties in the garden, such as Mo had been to on his first night at No.31, but often the witches would prefer to go to a disco. Off they would go into the night and find a dance hall where Boum! Boum! Boum! was coming into the air. Down they would swoop, leave their broomsticks in the car park, dive into the disco and dance till dawn. A whole group of witches certainly made the dancing wild!

And when it was over their sticks would carry them to their windows. They would stagger through and fall fast asleep on their beds.

———————

ooOoo

They would dive into the disco and dance until dawn

CHAPTER THIRTEEN

Elor

One day Zanzi was sipping her tea in bed when she said to Mo "I'm going out today. I'm going to a conference. A teachers' conference. I'm going straight after breakfast and coming back at teatime. I want you to watch the class for me. There will be another witch in charge. As for the afternoon you can have it off."

Mo was surprised to think that Zanzi would leave him while she went off. Who knew what he might get up to!

"They don't expect animals to accompany teachers - and the hotel doesn't allow them" she said by way of explanation. "But you'll never be able to get that globe out of my cabinet, so put that right out of your head. And you needn't try running away either."

Mo was pleased at least to think he could have a free afternoon.

++++++++

After breakfast Zanzi, Melda and Drine, all dressed in, not black witches' robes but in neat grey jackets and pleated skirts, went off in the car, cat No. 2 at the wheel in a grey chauffeur's uniform. He would, of course, stay well away from the hotel and do whatever chauffeurs did when they were not driving.

Mo waved them all good-bye and then went along to Zanzi's classroom. What a noise was there! Chairs being scraped along the floor, little feet scampering about, giggling and shouting. Who was in there? Mo opened the door and saw the three little hours running about, throwing what looked to be halved potatoes into the waste paper bins. Their faces were covered in paint. One, a little girl, No. 4, was eating a potato covered in blue.

Mo also saw - Elor.

Surely, he thought, they haven't put Elor in charge of the class!

71

What a noise was there !

But they had! Elor was sitting at the teacher's desk saying "Children! Please be quiet! Sit down! Order, please!"

The children were taking no notice of her. But, as soon as they saw Mo they ran to their desks and sat quietly.

"Good morning, Elor! Good morning, children! What are you learning this morning?"

The children did not reply.

Elor's desk was covered with large sheets of drawing paper, bottles of paint with little trays, and by her side was a box of potatoes.

"They're doing stencil painting with potatoes" said Elor in place of the children. "I'm cutting patterns on the potatoes, then they dip their potato into the paint and stamp it on their drawing paper. And the pattern comes out in colour."

'Well I'm glad she's not trying to teach them any magic' thought Mo. 'Anyway she couldn't if she tried!'

He picked up one of the halved potatoes. Aloud he said "It all looks very interesting, Elor."

"Yes. I'll give them some more paper and another potato and then we can get started."

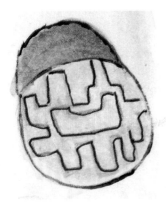

The pattern was very complicated

While Elor was giving out the potatoes, more paint and paper, Mo looked at the potato in his paw. The pattern was very complicated, all twisty and wavy lines 'Yet Elor can't cut her turnip lanterns straight. How has she done this?'

He went round to the children and looked at their potatoes. The patterns were wonderful - snowflakes, maze patterns, snakes and ladder patterns. Faces - cats, dogs, monkeys. Wonderful!

"These patterns are very good, Elor" said Mo.

"Yes, aren't they?"

73

She smiled at him. "It's my knife really". It makes all the difference when the knife is right."

She picked up a small knife with a black handle which was lying on her desk. "I had to buy this one specially from my catalogue, like my paintbrush. They're much better from my catalogue. This knife can cut anything. I'm going to use it on my turnip lantern tonight."

"Well, you can certainly be proud of what it does for your patterns" said Mo. So that was why Elor's flowers were so good. She did have a special paintbrush! And now she had a special knife! He wondered if the other witches knew about the catalogue.

The children made some lovely coloured snowflakes and other coloured patterns, and were quite happy and well-behaved for the rest of the lesson. If one of them began to fidget for any reason Mo would go and stand behind him and say a few words about his lovely artwork and the child would settle again.

At the end of the class the children handed in their papers and left the room. Elor gathered everything up in a big black bag, including the box of potatoes. Mo offered to carry the bag for her. "Oh no, Mo" said Elor, "it's quite all right. I can manage. The bag is really too heavy for you. I'm so glad you came into the class. I don't know what I would have done without you."

"Oh. Glad I was able to help" said Mo.

Elor went with her bag to the door. "Good-bye" she said. "See you at the party tonight."

Mo said good-bye. He was just about to leave the classroom himself when his gaze chanced to fall on the teacher's desk. Scatterbrain Elor! Her knife was still lying on the desktop. She had forgotten to put it in her bag.

He was about to run after her with it when an idea came into his head. He didn't run after Elor. He picked up the knife and ran upstairs instead.

---

ooOoo

CHAPTER FOURTEEN

The magic lock

Cautiously Mo entered Zanzi's room. Who knew what magic she had put upon the place while she was away! He walked to the cabinet. The Zebek globe still lay there on the top shelf in the corner, surrounded by little teddies. He bent down to look at the keyhole. Yes it was blocked. No hole there at all.

He looked at the knife he was carrying.

'Can cut anything. Hm! Well, here goes!'

He tried to prise the keyhole with the knife. Could it cut through the magic blocking material?

The knife moved by itself as he held it in his paw. Little bits of the keyhole fell out onto the floor. Mo took the knife away from the lock and looked into the keyhole again. Yes there was a space now. Quickly he ran to Zanzi's wardrobe, opened the door and took the small key he had noticed before. He thought it was a good thing Zanzi hadn't locked her wardrobe. He would have had to use the knife on that as well.

When he got back to the keyhole he got a shock!. He couldn't see the hole he had made. The magic material had re-formed itself!

He tried the knife again. And again. Before he had time to put the key in the lock the magic material blocked the hole again! What could he do?

Mo stood for a few minutes staring at the keyhole, blocked as ever it was. And yet the knife had been able to free it for a second or two.

He stood in front of the keyhole for a long time, thinking.

Slowly an idea formed in his mind. Why not try the knife and key together?

So that's exactly what he did. With the knife and key in the keyhole together the magic material was not able to re-form.

'And' thought Mo,'I can try a bit of magic myself.'

He had learned a lot while he had been with Zanzi.

So Mo stood in front of the cabinet and said

"Little key, little key,

Open now this door for me."

Silence.

Then after what seemed to Mo to be ages he heard a click and the door - was open!

Trembling Mo reached out his paw to take the globe. He was trembling because he thought he might turn into a frog on the spot. Would Zanzi have put any magic on the globe? Or was it too strong for her magic? Or did she think her magic on the lock was enough?

Mo wasn't going to stay long enough to find out. Once he had the globe he seized his little bag from its hook in Zanzi's wardrobe, hung the key on its rack and put the globe into his bag. He took the knife out of the lock and laid it on the floor. He closed the door of the cabinet and sure enough within a few seconds the magic material in the keyhole had re-formed itself.

Mo put his bag on his shoulder, strode to the windowsill, opened the window and was just about to open his mouth when he remembered

'The knife!'

He ran back and picked it up off the floor 'I must give it back to Elor!'

He ran downstairs and all the way to the flower painting class. "You left your knife in the classroom" he said to Elor, and he put the knife on her table.

"Thank you, Mo" said Elor, And she waved her paintbrush in his direction.

Mo ducked in case any magic sparks flew off it and said "Cheers, Elor!"

Then he ran upstairs again back to Zanzi's bedroom. He rushed to the windowsill again. Through the open window he said "Come, broomstick, come!"

And a broomstick came and Mo got on it. "Go, go, go!" he said. And he was away!

ooOoo

CHAPTER FIFTEEN

Where Next?

Mo was away on the broomstick through the pleasant afternoon, enjoying his freedom - until he remembered that Zanzi had warned him about running away.

For an instant his courage failed. 'I don't want to be a frog' he thought.

The broomstick dipped and swerved. 'Think of something else!' he told himself hastily.

Mo thought of Elor. Her turnip lanterns would improve and she would be all right if Zanzi didn't find out about the knife.......

The broomstick righted itself again. Mo noticed that he was flying over a house where people were making preparations for a big bonfire, carrying bundles of sticks,

A guy in a red and white scarf

and broken down old chairs to put on the pile. Some children were pulling a cart in which was a guy in a red and white scarf and a bowler hat.

'I think I should turn left now' thought Mo, and he ordered the broomstick to "No. 1. Janazar."

It was not long before Mo was landing in the garden at Janus' house. He tapped on the door with the broomstick as he could not reach the knocker and hoped the stick wouldn't mind. He also hoped that

Janus was at home.

The door opened. The butler showed him into the long hall again where Janus was already sitting."You found a Zebek globe" he said. "Please let me look at it."

Mo plunged his paw in his bag and found thankfully that the globe was still in it. He gave it to Janus who held it in the palm of his hand and considered it thoughtfully."It was never under the hats" he said.

A long pause. Then "I can't solve the puzzle. You'll have to take it to someone else." Janus gave the globe back to Mo.

"But who? And Zanzi will be back at teatime!"

Janus pressed his fingertips together, thinking very serious thoughts. The he snapped his fingers and his manservant appeared.

"Tell cook to wrap up one of the spare Christmas puddings in gift paper and get it brought up here."

To Mo he said "I want you to take a present to 25 Yule."

Christmas presents! thought Mo, when he was in danger of being turned into a frog! Janus got up from his chair, said "Good-bye, Mo!" and walked out of the room.

Then just as Mo was feeling hopelessly lost he returned. "Don't eat anything" he said.

And that was the moment the butler gave Mo a box wrapped in gold and silver gift paper.

Janus spoke again "Play the games and you'll be free. All then shall unravelled be."

Then he was gone. Mo was all alone in the hall. Checking that his globe was in his bag, his gold and silver box under his arm, he left the house. The broomstick had gone!

ooOoo

CHAPTER SIXTEEN

Danger!

Yule was of course not far from where Mo was. He just walked down a path running by the railway line and there was the entrance to the street. It was quiet, cold, but on the whole cheerful, much more cheerful than the street he had left. Windows were lit by Christmas trees and folk in the street were exchanging greetings. It was also bin day. All the houses had their dustbins on the pavement.

Mo hurried along as quickly as he could, not stopping to greet anyone. The darkness was falling - there were shadows all around.

And a shadow overhead! Three large black shadows! Mo jumped quickly over a low wall belonging to one of the houses and crouched down, hardly able to breathe. Yes, the shadow was Zanzi! And Melda. And Drine.

Three broomsticks swished to earth.

"What makes you think he's here, Zanzi?"

"I saw him at the top of the road. He's here all right."

Zanzi began poking around in a hollybush at the side of the wall, not far from Mo.

"Well, you won't be able to smell him out here because it's too cold." (Witches have a very good sense of smell).

"That's true" said Zanzi. And she lifted the lid of the dustbin that stood by the gate.

"He could be in any one of these bins" said Drine. She was going to look in the bins on the other side of the street when Melda said "There's no point in hunting for him in the bins. It would take too long and people would think we were after their rubbish."

79

"If you want it you'll have to take it"

"They wouldn't dare stop us" said Zanzi.

"Well, I'm not going through rubbish" said Melda.

"You'll do as I say!" said Zanzi.

Drine was not too happy about going through rubbish either but she tried to stop Zanzi from getting in a temper.

"I don't think he's in this street at all. Why don't we try Cat Safety? I'll bet that's where he is."

"Cat Safety in Janazar?" said Zanzi. She frowned "I suppose he could have cut back there. No - " she shook her head - "He's here. I know it!"

And she looked over the wall.

"I was right, wasn't I, girls?" she said with glee. "Hiding behind the wall! Come on, let's be having you!"

She grabbed Mo by the fur on the back of his neck and lifted him up over the wall and onto the pavement.

"Onto the broomstick with you!"

She noticed the gold and silver box. "What's that you're carrying? Give it to me!"

Mo felt angry. He did not want to go home with Zanzi and she was far too bossy.

"It's for 25 Yule. And I'm not going to give it to you! If you want it you'll have to take it!"

There was a sudden silence from the witches.

"25 Yule?" said Zanzi slowly. Mo felt her fingers slide off his neck as she dropped her hand to her side.

She stood absolutely still. Melda clapped her hand to her mouth.

"You can't touch it, Zanzi" said Drine. "Not if it's for there!". She seemed a bit afraid.

Zanzi's jaw had dropped at least two centimetres. She stayed silent for at least another minute. When she spoke at last her voice was very quiet.

"And I can't touch him either. He's got his globe out of my cabinet and I can't touch him!"

Mo could hardly believe his ears! These witches could do anything with magic!

There they were, all three of them looking down at Mo, not saying a word. He stood there silent too, his parcel clutched under his arm.

Zanzi was like an angry wasp. Mo could feel how angry she was. The world stood still for a moment.

Mo heard a whisper from Melda "25 Yule!" she said letting out a breath.

"25 Yule!" whispered Drine, with fear in her voice.

Zanzi's anger seemed to drain away and again she became quite still like a stone. After what was to Mo a very long time she said to Melda and Drine "I have no choice."

To Mo she said "You were quite a good pal, you know. I'll let you off!"

And she climbed upon her broomstick and swung away into the night far up into the sky. So did Melda. So did Drine. Soon all three were just little specks in the night sky.

Someone wished Mo a happy Christmas.

ooOoo

Soon all three were little specks in the sky

82

CHAPTER SEVENTEEN

At 25 Yule.

Mo continued on his way through Yule. He felt he'd just had a very narrow escape. The people who lived at No. 25 must be very special indeed!

He reached the door of the house, which was built like a castle and had rows of twinkling coloured lights strung up in the garden, and rang the bell.

The door was opened by two children, 8 and 10. Mo recognised their green costumes and holly badges as being just the same as those of the three who, oh so long ago, had taken his horse. He began to feel a bit more cheerful. This looked to be a nice house. And maybe his horse was in it!

"Come in, Mo. Merry Christmas!"

Mo was surprised to learn they knew his name but all he said was "I've brought you a present".

"Goodee!"

Four hands reached out for the gold and silver parcel. "Come with us while we put it on the Tree!"

Mo followed the children into a very long panelled room at the end of which was the largest Christmas tree he had ever seen. Children were all over the room, this time all dressed in red and green. All had holly badges.

A ladder leaned against the Tree on which stood No.12. decorating the Tree in gold and silver ribbon. No. 9 was up another ladder hanging a model aeroplane.

Mo's gift was passed to No. 12 who hung it on the other side of the Tree.

Someone clapped his hands and a big voice said "Now children, shall we show Mo how to play a few games!"

Mo turned from the Tree to see a huge figure with a white beard, clothes all red, boots very black and shiny, seated at one side of a big log fire, drinking something out of a mug. (No prizes for guessing who he was).

"Have a mince pie!" the figure said to Mo and waved his mug at a large table piled with food.

Mo suddenly felt very hungry. But he didn't much like mince pies.

No, thank you, Sir."

Then he noticed some lovely slices of turkey and chicken. He was about to ask if he could have some when Janus' warning about eating came into his head.

"I'd like to play a game, Sir."

"Good, good", said Santa (Yes, you were right) "let's play 'Santa says'."

On the other side of the tree

The children formed a circle, drawing Mo into it. It was soon clear to Mo that 'Santa says' was in fact the same as 'Simon says.'

"Santa says 'Clap your hands'."

Everybody clapped their hands.

"Touch your toes!" Aha, the few who did touch their toes were out because the command wasn't one of Santa's.

The game began again. "Shut your eyes!" More out because Santa had not said.

Mo found that he was the winner of the game.

"The winner can be blind man first" said Santa. And Mo was put in the centre of another circle and a

84

blindfold was put over his eyes. He could not see a thing!

He was spun round by several pairs of hands and then he was on his own.

He clutched at scraps of silken clothing and they slid from his paws. He touched a lock of hair and it was gone. There was giggling, and scuttling noises, and puffs of breath blown in his face. His paws met empty air.

Mo was getting a bit dizzy. He stopped chasing and took off his blindfold.

The room was empty! Except for the Tree and the table loaded with food. But the giggling was still going on. People were still there, all there, but he couldn't see them. He felt someone open his bag and take out the globe. He put in his paw. Yes, the bag was empty. The he saw, actually saw, the globe sail through the air and land on a branch of the Tree where it perched magically. Mo thought 'Well, they can't make the globe invisible, only themselves!'

He was standing in the centre of the room. Suddenly one of the big doors in the hall opened. Outside them Mo could just see in the corner of the open door something that could be - the rockers of a rocking-horse! He heard the sound of a window opening.

'It's there!' said Mo excitedly to himself. 'It's there!' He could hardly keep from dancing up and down. 'It's either started moving again or someone has brought it!'

But how to get to it? And he must get his globe back.

"Please, Sir, can I have my globe back?" asked Mo.

The model aeroplane separated itself from the Tree and glided to his feet.

"Please - my globe. If you don't mind, Sir."

The gold and silver parcel left the Tree and came to rest at Mo's feet.

Suddenly Mo knew how to do it!

"'Santa says Please give me, Mo, my globe back!'"

There was a burst of hearty laughter and the globe, the precious Zebek globe, left its perch on the Tree and slid to Mo's feet. Quickly he picked it up and stuffed it in his bag, and fastened the flap securely.

"Thank you, Sir!" he said, and bowed.

Then they made a pathway through themselves to the door

But now he had to get out of the house. He could feel people coming closer, hands ruffling the fur on the top of his head, little tweaks of his tail.

"'Santa says, CAN MO HAVE HIS HORSE BACK?'"

There was a great silence throughout the hall which lasted for all of a minute . Mo hardly dared to breathe.

Santa and the children suddenly became visible again. They were all around him, silent. They started clapping their hands.

And then they made a pathway through themselves to the door where Mo wanted to go. He walked quickly through the throng of boys and girls.

When he got to the door he said "Thank you!"

Then he turned and jumped onto the horse's back. He patted his bag to make sure the globe was safe. Then decided to look inside. What a shock he got! The globe was glowing and shining inside the bag. There was a lot of whirring and clicking going on! What was happening?

The whirring and clicking finally stopped. Mo put his paw inside the bag. Carefully he felt the globe. It seemed all right. He pulled it out. It was no longer glowing and shining. But! It was no longer jumbled! The colours were all matching! Each colour was grouped together and made five perfect coloured parts! Wonderful!

Mo heard Santa's voice saying "What next, Mo?"

"To the summerhouse!" he commanded the horse.

The horse began to move. Mo quickly put the globe back into his bag.

"Goodbye! Goodbye, Mo!" said Santa and the children.

"Goodbye!" said Mo.

He pulled the mane. "Go fast!" he shouted "Go as fast as you can!"

The horse made straight for the open window and went high, high into the air...... and came down outside the summerhouse in the Dream country. Dorinda's summerhouse.

Quickly Mo ran inside and went straight to the windowsill where he had first found the globe. He took it out of his bag, all perfect, and put it back on the exact spot where he had taken it from. It looked fine!

Then he rushed outside, got on the horse again and said "Home! Home!"

Then everything went black.

---

ooOoo

When he got to the door Mo said "Thank you"

CHAPTER EIGHTEEN

Home at Last!

Mo came to his senses on Aunt Daffodil's lounge carpet, the rocking-horse by his side. Aunt Daffodil was looking down at him, patting his paw.

"Oh, thank goodness you're coming round now!"

"It was Christmas Day" Mo said faintly.

"Yes, it was. But it isn't now. It's summer."

Mo took a glance through the french windows and saw the sun shining on all the flowers.

Aunt Daffodil was in a very good mood. "You did it, Mo! You did it!"

"Did I?" asked Mo, not really being sure of things. "What did I do?" He hoped he had done something, for it had been a very long trip.

Aunt Daffodil replied excitedly. "You changed the Zebek globe!"

"I did?" said Mo.

"All Dorinda's toys are still there at the back of her mind. She remembers every single one. She was given the Zebek globe by one of her father's prime ministers. It was specially made for her, and like no other."

Mo remembered. Dorinda wouldn't let him try to fix it and she couldn't fix it on her own, so the globe was forgotten, pushed to the back of a cupboard.

"We couldn't fix it" said Mo.

"No. When she fell asleep she still remembered the globe all jumbled up. We wanted to wake her up again, didn't we?"

"Yes" said Mo.

"So" went on Aunt Daffodil "we had to break Henbane's spell. You've done that!"

"How?" asked Mo.

"By changing the globe! Dorinda doesn't remember it jumbled up any more - she remembers it perfect!"

"Ah," said Mo. "She has the perfect globe in the summerhouse!"

"That's right. I knew when Dorinda fell asleep she would remember the globe still as jumbled. I managed to move it from the cupboard to the windowsill where you would find it. Now it's perfect and the spell is broken! If Dorinda sees any more pills they won't matter at all!"

"But I didn't do anything!" said Mo. "It was Santa who changed the globe!"

"Oh, You did everything, Mo. You had so many struggles in that strange country and they all worked for Dorinda. Even Santa couldn't have done it without you!"

Mo thought about all his adventures - about the Tortoise, about Jay, about Janus, about the Fool, about Zanzi, about Elor, (particularly about Elor) and about Santa, and said

"They all happened then?"

"Yes" said Aunt Daffodil. "They all happened. And it's all over now. I think you'll find when you get home that everyone has woken up. So let's both have a nice cup of tea!"

The End

ooOoo